St. W9-CTR-491

WOMEN OF THE WEST

👆 A family stands proudly outside their home on the frontier, 1870s.

WOMEN
OF THE WEST

SUSAN KATZ KEATING

Dedication:
To my own little wild women: Erin, Kelly and Courtney

Mason Crest Publishers
370 Reed Road
Broomall PA 19008
www.masoncrest.com

First printing

1 3 5 7 9 8 6 4 2

Library of Congress Cataloging-in-Publication Data
on file at the Library of Congress

ISBN 1-59084-069-0

Publisher's note: many of the quotations in this book come from
original sources, and contain the spelling and grammatical
inconsistencies of the original text.

CONTENTS

👆 Travelling with the covered wagon trains of the Mormons was one way frontier women made their way West. It was often a grueling and lonely journey, and there was not much to greet the pioneers upon their arrival in the undeveloped western territories.

ON THE FRONTIER

FOURTEEN-YEAR-OLD MARGARET MCNEIL
WAS SETTING UP CAMP FOR THE NIGHT.
She had walked all day along the Mormon Trail, from
Nebraska to Salt Lake City, in what is now Utah. The
whole way, Margaret carried her little brother James
on her back. James was four years old, and he was sick
with measles.

Margaret and James were tired and hungry. They
missed their mother, who was in a different group
that was also crossing the plains. Now, after a long
day's walk, the two McNeil youngsters would finally
be able to rest and eat.

But that night, the cow ran away. Margaret jumped up to
catch the cow; she did not even stop to put on her shoes.
She knew that without the cow, there would be no milk.
Later, Margaret wrote, "Had it not been for the milk, we
would have starved."

In her race to catch the cow, Margaret did not pay
attention to where she was going. "All of a sudden I began to
feel I was walking on something soft," Margaret wrote. "I
looked down to see what it could be, and to my horror found

👆 Sacagawea (sometimes spelled Sacajawea) is shown here with Meriwether Lewis and William Clark. Sacagawea was the wife of a member of Lewis and Clark's 1804–06 expedition. She helped guide the American explorers through the northwest to the Pacific Ocean and back to St. Louis.

that I was standing in a bed of snakes, large ones and small ones." Margaret was petrified. "At the sight of them I became so weak I could scarcely move," she wrote.

It was a terrible experience, even for a brave girl like Margaret. But it was neither the worst thing nor the most frightening thing that happened to a woman in the Old West.

Sacagawea, the Indian guide for the Lewis and Clark expedition, nearly drowned with her baby in a flood.

Virginia Reed, a young pioneer, watched her companions starve to death while trapped for an entire winter in the snowbound Sierra Nevada Mountains. Clara Brown, a former slave who worked for years to earn enough money to buy property, lost three of her houses in a fire.

In 2000, the U.S. Mint issued a gold dollar coin featuring the likeness of Sacagawea carrying her baby, Jean-Baptiste, on her back. It was the first time a child was portrayed on a circulating American coin.

In the Old West, women learned to endure these types of hardships. They did not like them, but they understood that such things could happen.

Along with the hardship came amazing adventure. In a time when many women were restricted by society's rules, women in the West lived remarkable lives. Indian guides like Sacagawea roamed the continent as interpreters for white explorers. Pioneer women rode across beautiful but hostile territory in rickety covered wagons. Some, like Margaret, walked the same distance, pushing their belongings in handcarts.

These women built homes and raised families in isolated wilderness. They took up arms alongside their men. They got rich. They went broke. Some even became outlaws.

In the Old West, a respectable woman was known as a "Sunbonnet Sue."

In August 1805, Lewis and Clark and their company (including Sacagawea, their Native American interpreter) encountered a tribe of Shoshone Indians who had never before seen white people. The two explorers desperately needed horses to carry supplies across the massive Continental Divide. They hoped to buy pack animals from the Shoshone herd.

At first, the Shoshones suspected that Lewis and Clark were planning to attack. Finally, after offering signs of peace, Lewis and Clark sat down with a group of Shoshones and their chief, Cameahwait, to talk about buying the horses. But the two groups needed an interpreter.

William Clark wrote in his journal: "Sacagawea was sent for; she came … sat down, and was beginning to interpret, when, in the person of Cameahwait, she recognized her brother." It was an amazing coincidence. Many years earlier, while still a young girl, Sacagawea had been kidnapped from the Shoshones by Hidatsa Indians. She had not seen her brother since. Now she was overjoyed. Wrote Clark: "She instantly jumped up, and ran and embraced him, throwing over him her blanket, and weeping profusely."

After that, the negotiations went very smoothly indeed. The chief sold Lewis and Clark as many horses as they needed. When the expedition left for the next leg of its great journey, the Shoshones begged Sacagawea to remain with them. She chose to go with Lewis and Clark.

No one is certain when Sacagawea died. Clark wrote that she became sick and died in 1812. However, some people think that she lived in Wyoming until 1886.

No matter how they lived their individual lives, all these women played an important part in the American West. They lived on the *frontier* of change. They helped open a strange new land for the nation. And in many ways, by forging new roles for themselves, they helped shape the lives of women who lived after them.

👆 During the 1840s, pioneer families crossed some of the roughest terrain in North America, hoping to find farmland in the west. Most followed the Oregon Trail, a series of paths that led from Missouri to the Oregon Territory in the northwest. This large region included the present-day states of Oregon, Washington, and Idaho.

MOTHERS OF THE WEST

FROM 1830 TO 1866, HUNDREDS OF THOUSANDS OF AMERICANS TRAVELED THE VAST COUNTRY and settled western territories that had not yet become states. Among the pioneers were **scores** of women who had many different reasons for joining the great **migration**.

Narcissa Whitman wanted to teach Christianity to Indians. She and her husband started a mission in Oregon Territory. Other women wanted to fulfill what they thought was the country's "manifest destiny," which means "clear purpose," or "clear fate." Like other Americans of their day, these women believed that people of European descent were destined by God to expand the nation all the way to the Pacific shore.

Mormon women, like Margaret McNeil, wanted to find a new western land where they could practice their religion in peace. Some women went west to become rich. Still others went for very personal reasons.

Clara Brown was a freed slave who traveled west hoping to find the daughter she had lost many years earlier. The daughter, Eliza Jane, had been sold at a slave auction in Kentucky. Clara

Many of the women who moved west found jobs as teachers. Schools were often plain and books scarce on the frontier, as this painting by Winslow Homer shows.

was heartbroken. Year in and year out, Clara—who was known as "Aunt" Clara Brown—searched tirelessly for Eliza Jane. Everywhere she went, Clara told people about Eliza Jane, hoping that someone might know where she was. Clara never gave up. Finally, after 47 years, Clara found her long-lost Eliza Jane. In the meantime, Clara had started churches in many communities. She was beloved by the thousands of former slaves she had helped.

Much is known about the lives of pioneer women because so many of them wrote letters and diaries. To this day, we can still read their words of hope and sorrow; fear and adventure.

Tabitha Brown was already a grandmother when, at age 66, she joined a wagon train that included her children,

grandchildren, and 74-year-old brother-in-law. In a letter to her brother and sister, Tabitha wrote that she had experienced so many adventures that her story "would fill a volume of many pages."

As did other pioneers, Tabitha saw many sudden tragedies on her journey west. A six-year-old boy fell from his family's wagon and was killed beneath the wheels. Another child died of scarlet fever, a disease that is easily cured today with **antibiotics**.

In 1859, "Aunt" Clara Brown allowed her home to be used for Methodist church services. The congregation became one of the first churches in Colorado, the St. James Methodist church in Central City.

Tabitha herself endured hardship and danger. After losing her wagon and all her belongings, the old woman found herself separated from the rest of the wagon train. She was forced to proceed on horseback accompanied only by her brother-in-law, a man named Captain Jack. The captain was so weak that he toppled off his own horse. Tabitha managed to get him back in the saddle, and then led the horse while Captain Jack sat doubled over, clinging to the animal's mane.

That night, Tabitha built a makeshift tent. She brought the feeble Captain Jack inside the flimsy shelter. "His senses were gone," Tabitha later wrote. "I covered him as well as I could with blankets, and then seated myself upon my feet behind him, expecting he would be a corpse by morning."

About 10 percent of the women who traveled west via covered wagon were teenaged girls. A traditional going-away gift from friends was a blank diary in which to write about the trip.

During the long night, Tabitha took stock of her situation. She was alone in the vast wilderness, cold and hungry, with not even the moon or starlight for comfort. "All was solitary as death," she wrote.

But morning brought new hope. Captain Jack was better, and another **emigrant** found the two old people and led them to his wagons. There, Tabitha learned that Indians had killed other white people during the night. It was chilling news. Earlier that morning, Tabitha had found fresh tracks just outside her tent. Did they belong to the Indians who had killed those other people? Tabitha must have wondered why she and Captain Jack were spared.

By the time Tabitha settled in Oregon, she had few belongings and no money. She did not know how she was going to support herself. Then, while trying to pluck what she thought was a button from the finger of a glove, Tabitha found a single coin. It was worth only about six cents.

With that coin, she bought needles from some Native American women. She traded the women her old clothes for some **buckskins**. She turned the skins into gloves and sold them. Before long, Tabitha had a thriving business.

But she was not content merely to support herself. Tabitha was greatly interested in the lives and well-being of other settlers. She was upset that so many children had been orphaned when their parents died on the Oregon Trail.

Along with two missionary friends, Harvey and Emmeline Clark, Tabitha built a log cabin home for orphans. There, Tabitha taught school and cared for the needy children. She also took in children who had been abandoned. The orphan

While the trip West was often dangerous, the hardship did not end when the pioneer families reached their destinations. Settlers had to contend with bad weather and often faced shortages of food and necessary items. Raids by Native Americans were also a common problem. These Minnesota settlers are fleeing from their homes because of a Sioux uprising in the early 1860s.

Tabitha Brown's trip west was "pleasing and prosperous," she wrote, until a "rascally fellow" advised her group to take a short cut. "The idea of shortening a long journey caused us to yield to his advice," Tabitha wrote in an 1854 letter to her brother and sister. "Our sufferings from that time no tongue could tell." The "short cut" added hundreds of miles and many months to the group's journey. "We had sixty miles desert without grass or water," Tabitha wrote. She went on to list the obstacles her group faced: "Mountains to climb, cattle giving out, wagons breaking, emigrants sick and dying, hostile Indians to guard against by night and by day to keep from getting killed, or having our horses and cattle arrowed or stolen."

While riding through one difficult pass, Tabitha saw dead cattle, broken wagons, and scattered goods. "Some people were in the Canyon two and three weeks before they could get through; some died without any warning from fatigue and starvation; others ate the flesh of the cattle that were lying dead by the wayside."

Tabitha was terrified. Still, the 66-year-old grandmother took pride in her bravery. She noted that she never cried nor gave up hope: "Through all my sufferings in crossing the Plains, I had not once sought relief by the shedding of tears, nor thought we should not live to reach the settlements."

school, which became known as the Tualatin Academy, was one of the first schools in the Northwest. Later, Tabitha used her own money to help construct a better building to replace the old log cabin. The "new" building, completed in 1850, is still standing. It is on the grounds of Pacific University in Salem, Oregon.

People in Oregon remember Tabitha Brown to this day. In 1987, the Oregon State legislature passed a resolution to honor her. They named her the "Mother of Oregon."

Not every pioneer woman did so many things or became so important. Some had a sad fate. Narcissa Whitman, the woman who came west hoping to teach Christianity to Native Americans, had problems at her mission. The Indians were happy with their own religion, and they did not want to be converted. Tension grew between the Whitmans and the Native Americans. When smallpox killed most of the Indian children, the Indians blamed Narcissa and her husband for spreading the disease. Narcissa and her husband were killed.

A great number of women, though, survived the early hardships of pioneer existence, and went on to live their lives. For instance, Margaret McNeil escaped her frightening encounter with the snakes. "All I could think of was to pray, and in some way I jumped out of them," she wrote of the night she found herself standing on top the serpents. "The Lord blessed and cared for me."

Margaret arrived safely in Utah. She got married there and raised 11 children. Like Tabitha Brown, Clara Brown, and Narcissa Whitman, Margaret and all the others who settled the new territory might simply be called, "Mothers of the West."

GOLD RUSH WOMEN

UNTIL 1849, MOST AMERICAN WOMEN LIVING IN THE WEST WERE EITHER NATIVE AMERICANS or pioneers who had traveled the Oregon Trail. But in 1849, something happened to cause big changes among women in the West—gold was discovered in California.

Hoping to get rich, people came to the "Promised Land" from all over. In just a few short years, more than 180,000 people swarmed into California. The new frontierswomen were **entrepreneurs**: a lively group of people who hoped to create new ways to earn a living.

Some of the women forty-niners, as they were called, came to California with their husbands to hunt for gold. Word spread that women as well as men were finding treasure. Harriet Behrins dug an ounce of gold from the

> Prospectors panned for gold in the rivers of North California. The technique required hours of discomfort, alertness, and patience. Some women tried to find their fortunes in the gold fields; other moved to San Francisco and other booming California cities to find jobs.

ground with a spoon. Another woman supposedly found a single gold rock worth $13,000.

Lucena Parsons wrote in her journal that she caught "gold fever." In one journal entry, she described the day's takings: "We again went to the canion [her spelling] to find that bewitching ore that is called gold. We had better luck in finding it to day, my husband and I making 16 dollars in fine dust."

Louisa Clapp, who called herself a mineress—meaning "lady miner"—wrote of the job's indignities: "I wet my feet, tore my dress, spoilt a pair of new gloves, nearly froze my fingers, got an awful headache, took cold and lost a valuable breast-pin, in this my labor of love."

Those who didn't actually search for gold themselves found ways to make money from the prospectors. Some women came west with their own stoves and pots. They earned good wages by washing clothes and cooking for the gold miners in their camps.

Luzena Wilson let the miners come to her. She first drove her wagon into Sacramento on an October evening in 1849, after a long trip. Not a penny was left in her pocket. All the family's money had fallen from the wagon the day before. "The nest egg was gone," Luzena later told her daughter, "but the homely bird which laid it—the power and the will to work—was still there."

Luzena and her family parked their wagon in "a wilderness of canvas tents," where the gold miners lived. A few days later, a man walked past Luzena's campfire. He offered her five dollars for a breakfast cooked by a woman. Luzena sold him the food, but she realized afterward that she could have asked double the price.

In 1849, men in Sacramento could not buy goods by promising to pay for them later. A woman was considered trustworthy, though, and was permitted to buy food on credit.

After three days in the tent city, Luzena and her husband were penniless no more. They had made enough money selling home-cooked meals to the miners that they sold their oxen and bought a hotel. The rooms soon filled and Luzena cooked more meals. She worked so hard that she barely had time even to say hello to her neighbors. "Yes, we worked," Luzena said years later. "We did things that our high-toned servants would now look at aghast, and say it was impossible for a woman to do. But the ones who did not work in '49 went to the wall."

Still, she enjoyed a high **_status_** in the community. "Women were scarce in those days," Luzena said. "I lived six months in Sacramento and saw only two." The men of the town treated Luzena with great respect, as though she were a rare and precious creature. They stopped cursing or fighting whenever she walked in the room. They tried to behave properly when she was near. Said Luzena: "I was a queen."

Clothing was a problem for women during the California Gold Rush. The long, flowing dresses of the day were not suited for the mines or for the muddy streets of San Francisco. Some women coped by wearing men's boots and clothing; others wore the controversial new pantaloons, called bloomers after their inventor, Amelia Bloomer.

Like Luzena, many other women in the gold rush days ran hotels and restaurants. Margaret Frink attracted customers by offering a special treat—milk. At the time, milk sold for two dollars per gallon. Margaret had her own cow, and could collect as much milk as the cow produced. Margaret set out free milk on the tables of her Frink's Hotel. She drew in many miners who had not had milk in a long time.

Women also made money by washing the miners' clothes. Incredibly, many miners had been sending their clothes to the Sandwich Islands or even to China to be washed. Then they waited months to get their clothes back. They were happy to pay high prices to have their clothes washed and returned quickly.

Other women took on unusual jobs. The unmarried "Charley" Parkhurst disguised herself as a man and became a stagecoach driver for Wells, Fargo & Company. Julia Shannon set up shop in San Francisco as a photographer and *midwife*.

In 1853, a young Irish girl named Marie Gilbert arrived in San Francisco on board ship. The beautiful Marie told people

☞ Irish-born American dancer Lola Montez raised the spirits of weary and desolate prospectors. For all the hype surrounding the California Gold Rush, it was often more profitable to offer goods or services to the miners than to be one.

that her name was Lola Montez. She said she was a dancer from Spain. "Lola Montez" began to do shows in San Francisco theaters. She became very well known. Other actresses even did shows imitating her.

"Lola" made friends with a six-year-old girl named Lotta Crabtree. Lotta and her mother Mary Ann had come west from New York to join Lotta's father John, who had been searching for gold.

When John's gold mining efforts brought little money, Mary Ann decided to see if Lotta could become famous like Lola Montez. Lotta took singing lessons and went to dancing school. Finally, Lotta was ready to do a performance. She dressed up in an Irish costume her mother had made. She sang for some miners at a saloon. The miners loved her so

Luzena Wilson and her family lived in a house made of canvas in Sacramento, California, about a mile from the American River. One day the **town crier** galloped by on his horse, warning, "The **levee**'s broke!" The river had broken its bounds. The men all ran to help repair the break. But their efforts, Luzena later told her daughter, were useless: "Their puny strength could do nothing against such a flood of waters."

Luzena looked out at the street and saw a wall of water headed her way. "Almost before I thought what it was," she said, "the water rushed against the door-sill at my feet." Within minutes, the water was six inches high inside the house. Luzena gathered her children and a few belongings. She waded through what was now a strong river in the street. She took refuge in a nearby hotel. As the waters continued to rise, Luzena and her family moved to an upper floor. "In an hour more the whole town was afloat, and the little boats were rowed here and there picking up the people and rescuing what could be saved of the property."

All that night, Luzena said, people were heard calling for help. Luzena and her family wound up in a group of 40 people sharing one long room, barely above the flood. "The water splashed upon the ceiling below, and the rain and the wind made the waves run high on this inland sea," she later wrote. Luzena and her fellow refugees stayed in the room for days, while the town remained partially flooded. Luzena's husband even built a floating floor for their house, so that the floor could rise and fall with the tide.

More than 30 years later, memories of the flood still haunted Luzena. She wrote, "I can not hear the sound of continuous rain without, in a measure, living over again the terrors of those monotonous days, and feel creeping over me the dread of the rising waters."

As a young
woman, Lotta
Crabtree made
her living
charming her way
into the hearts of
miners as a singer
and dancer in
saloons and
mining camps.

much they threw gold nuggets onto the stage.

Soon, Lotta Crabtree began traveling to the mining camps, where she sang and danced for the miners. Always, the men rewarded Lotta with gold dust or nuggets. The little girl was a star. She was known as "Miss Lotta, the San Francisco Favorite." By the time she died, in 1924 at the age of 77, Lotta Crabtree owned property worth $4 million. This was a huge fortune, one that could be traced to a young woman's part in the California gold rush.

LAW MAKERS, LAW BREAKERS

ON MAY 29, 1899, A STAGECOACH CARRYING
THREE PASSENGERS RUMBLED THROUGH THE
Dripping Spring Mountains in Arizona. Two bandits suddenly
appeared out of nowhere, and forced the driver to stop. The
bandits stole every penny the stagecoach passengers had, but
one of the robbers then had a twinge of guilt. Taking pity on
the people who had just been robbed, the bandit gave each
trembling victim one dollar for food—and then took off in a
cloud of dust.

The stage robbers didn't get far before the sheriff caught
them. It turned out that the softhearted bandit who had given
each victim a dollar was a woman. She was Pearl Hart.

Belle Starr, the infamous bandit queen, poses here
holding a pistol. With more freedom available to them in
the West than back east, women sometimes found
themselves on the wrong side of the law.

This statue of Esther Hobart Morris stands in front of the Wyoming State Capitol building in Cheyenne. Not only was she a formidable women's rights proponent, she also served as the first female justice of the peace in the U.S.

People were shocked. A couple of women in Texas and Oklahoma had already become deputy U.S. *marshals*, proving that women were not necessarily the weaker sex, but still, people were amazed that a woman had robbed a stagecoach.

The first known instance of a woman casting a vote in America was in 1805, when explorers Lewis and Clark included their Native American guide, Sacagawea, when polling the expedition members on where to spend the winter.

Brash and beautiful, the 29-year-old Pearl created an even bigger stir when she announced that she would not go to court. Pearl argued

that because only men had written the laws, the law applied only to men. She refused to be tried under a law no woman had made. This was a quite a twist on the heated topic of women's rights. All across the country, people were already debating whether women should be able to own property; keep the money they worked for; and vote in elections. People who supported women's rights were called suffragists.

In the east, the suffragists made slow progress. But in the West, where women had struggled alongside men to establish the new frontier, change came more quickly. Long before all American women earned the right to vote, western women gained much ground toward becoming full citizens.

One of the first western women to push for women's rights was Esther Morris. In 1869, Esther and her family moved

Abigail S. Duniway, an Oregon pioneer and suffragist, supported women's issues through her writing. She also campaigned for women's rights, and lived her life as an example for other women to follow.

to the Wyoming Territory. Esther was very much interested in politics. She convinced the ***legislator*** from her district to introduce a law that granted women the right to vote. The law was passed.

In 1870, Esther was appointed ***justice of the peace*** for South Pass City. No other woman in America had held that type of job before. That same year, women in the Wyoming Territory served on ***juries*** for the first time in history.

Winema, a Native American woman who married a white miner, was not officially connected to any courts or agencies, but she too played a role in keeping the peace during difficult times. For years, Winema worked as a translator between whites and Modoc Indians who had been forced off their own lands in northern California.

In 1873, Winema warned the members of a U.S. peace delegation that Modoc leaders planned to kill them. The warning was ignored, and the U.S. delegation's leader was killed. Winema was able to save the life of one delegation member, Albert Meacham. Afterward, Winema and her family toured the country with Meacham, giving talks about the Modoc Indians.

The Winema National Forest in South Central Oregon is named for Winema, the Native American woman who hoped for peace between whites and the Modoc Indian tribe.

Meanwhile, back in the Wyoming Territory, Esther Morris was determined that when Wyoming became a state, women would still have the right to vote. In 1890, Esther's wish came true. Wyoming became the first state in the union where women could vote.

In Oregon, women's rights caught the attention of Abigail Scott Duniway. Abigail had come to Oregon at age 17. There, she became a schoolteacher and a farm wife. When her husband was injured and could no longer support the family, Abigail started her own business.

Abigail was very creative, and she wrote poetry and novels. The novels were about strong, capable women like herself. Abigail also started her own newspaper, called the *New Northwest*. She published chapters from her novels in the newspaper, and she also printed articles about women's rights.

Abigail made friends with one of the most famous American suffragettes, Susan B. Anthony. Abigail and Susan **campaigned** for women's rights. Abigail tried especially hard

Another notorious outlaw of the West was Flo Quick. She dressed as a man and called herself Tom King, rustling cattle in the Indian Territory during the 1880s.

Flo fell in love with Bob Dalton, who with his brothers Emmett and Gratton formed the Dalton Gang in 1890 and began to rob trains. Flo helped with their criminal activities. She would charm railroad workers into giving her information about the trains the Dalton Gang planned to rob. She also stole five horses for the Daltons to use to rob two banks in Coffeyville, Kansas. However, this plan backfired as Bob Dalton and three other gang members were killed during the attempt.

After this, Flo organized a gang of train robbers, but she soon dropped out of sight. She may have been killed in a gunfight.

to win women's **suffrage** for the states that had made up the former Oregon Territory: Oregon, Washington, and Idaho.

Like Esther Morris, Abigail saw her wish come true. Oregon, Washington, and Idaho all granted women the right to vote long before national law granted this right to women in 1920.

But while women such as Esther Morris and Abigail Scott Duniway worked to create laws, other women in the West were busy breaking laws. One of the most notorious outlaws of the Old West was the wild-living Myra Maybelle Starr. A pistol-packing horse thief, Myra was better known as Belle Starr, the Bandit Queen.

Belle came from a wealthy family in Missouri. Belle's father owned a stable and a blacksmith shop, and the family lived in

their own hotel. As a young girl, Belle was an excellent student.
She loved to go riding and shooting with her brother Bud.

But the Civil War was hard on Belle's family. Bud was
killed, and Belle's father lost his business. After the war, the
family moved to Texas, hoping to build a new life.

For Belle, the new life included bad company. In 1866, just
one year after the war ended, Belle befriended Cole Younger, a
member of the James Gang. She also became friends with
Jesse James. She married James Reed, the first of many
husbands, who later also became an outlaw.

Belle Starr had a daughter with Cole Younger, a
member of the infamous James Gang. Cole is seated at the
center of the gang in this 1870 photograph at their
mountain hideout in Missouri.

Pearl Hart became famous while being held in jail for robbing a stagecoach. Newspaper reporters wanted to hear the story of the lady bandit. Pearl told the reporters that she robbed the stagecoach while under great duress. According to Pearl, she had been mining in Arizona when she received a letter saying that her mother was dying.

Desperate for money to buy her passage home, Pearl and her companion Joe Boot decided to rob the stagecoach. "That letter drove me crazy," Pearl later wrote. "From what I know now, I believe I became temporarily insane." Still, Pearl did not want to stay in jail. She and another inmate escaped from jail in Tucson. She was caught and brought back for trial. She was sentenced to five years in the Territorial Prison in Yuma, Arizona.

There, she became even more famous. More reporters came. Photographers wanted to take pictures of her holding a gun. The popular Pearl was let out of prison two years early. Much later, when her legal troubles were over, Pearl went on tour. She appeared on stage in men's clothing, telling tales of her wild life of crime.

When a **bounty hunter** killed her husband Jim, Belle married another outlaw, Sam Starr. Belle and Sam lived in a cabin on Indian Territory. Belle and Sam's outlaw friends used to come to the cabin and hide out from whomever was chasing them.

Many wild stories are told about Belle Starr. In one story, she looped a rope around a man's neck and hoisted him up a tree until he revealed where he had hidden a $30,000 treasure. In another story, Belle was running from an angry *posse* when she came up with a plan to throw her pursuers off track. She told a ***blacksmith*** to nail her horse's shoes on backward, so that the posse would not know which direction she was traveling. Other tales say that Belle robbed a bank, burned down a store, robbed a poker game, and much more.

It is impossible to know whether these stories are true. But the records show that Belle was arrested in 1882 for stealing a horse. This was a serious crime in the Old West, but probably because she was a woman, Belle got off lightly. She was sentenced to only one year in jail. Later, however, she had other run-ins with the law. She was charged with robbery and horse theft. Each time, she was found not guilty.

After her husband Sam was killed in a shoot-out, Belle married a man named Bill July. Her new husband was not much older than her teenaged son, Eddie.

In 1889, Belle was shot in the back while riding home from a friend's house. The suspects included one of her friends, her husband, and even her own children. Her killer was never found. But Belle became a legend. People could not stop talking about the Bandit Queen.

Nor could they stop talking about the 1899 stagecoach robber, Pearl Hart, who refused to be tried under a law no woman had made. But this was one area where women had rights equal to men. Like it or not, Pearl had to stand trial. She was convicted and sent to jail.

👆 This postcard illustrates a cowgirl ready for the roundup. Many women of the west found their calling in professions usually occupied by men.

5

WILD WOMEN AND COWGIRLS

THE WEST GREW FASTER AND FASTER. CHANGE WAS ALWAYS IN THE AIR, AND LIFE WAS BOTH exciting and dangerous. People knew that anything could happen. Some of the most interesting wild people of the day were women.

Mary Fields was a 200-pound former slave who smoked cigars, dressed like a man, and carried a pistol. Mary was big and tough and liked to fight. She was known for being able to knock a man down with one punch. People said she could take on any two men in Montana Territory.

But if Mary was rough, she was also kind. She was good friends with a group of Catholic nuns in Montana. The head nun, Mother Amadeus, had been Mary's friend in childhood, and as an adult, Mary worked for Mother Amadeus and the nuns. Mary washed their clothes, cared for their chickens, and did much of the heavy work around the convent where the nuns lived.

Once, when Mary was gone for a few days, the nuns did Mary's chores. They burned a pile of her trash, not realizing

26 Calamity Jane, Notorious Frontier Character,
Gen. Crook's Scout.

👆 A colored postcard of Calamity Jane, one of the most famous women of the West. Stories and legends about her were printed in numerous dime novels, cheap books that were popular in the second half of the 19th century. Other subjects of dime novels included Buffalo Bill Cody, Billy the Kid, Jesse James, and Wild Bill Hickok. However, most of the stories in these books were tall tales.

that the trash contained live bullets. The bullets exploded like fireworks, and one of the nuns was accidentally injured. The nuns did not burn Mary's trash again.

Outside of the convent, Mary continued to get into fights. People in the town complained that she caused trouble. Finally, the bishop said that Mary Fields was too wild for the convent. She would have to leave.

Cowboy artist Charlie Russell used Montana wild woman Mary Fields as a model for one of his drawings. *A Quiet Day in Cascade* shows Mary being knocked over by a rampaging hog.

Mother Amadeus found a job for her longtime friend. Although the position was considered to be man's work, Mary was accepted as a mail carrier. Mother Amadeus even bought Mary a wagon and a team of horses to use on her route.

Mary ran the mail route for eight years. Once, the horses ran away with Mary in the wagon. Mary was badly hurt; but she blamed herself for losing control of the team.

When Mary finally stopped driving the mail route, she opened a restaurant in the town of Cascade, Montana. She also ran a laundry service. As an old woman, she still had the same personality: she fought from time to time, but she was known for her kindness, especially to people who were down on their luck. If people did not have enough money to pay for meals, Mary let them eat at her restaurant anyway.

When Calamity Jane died, people came to the funeral parlor to take her picture and cut off locks of her hair to keep as souvenirs.

The children of Cascade loved Mary. On her birthday, the school closed while Mary and the children celebrated.

When Mary was very old, a local hotel promised to provide her meals free for the rest of her life. Many people were very sad when she died in 1914 at age 82. For years afterward, people remembered the former slave who had become a wild woman of the West.

An even wilder woman was Martha Jane Cannary. Few people know her by that name, though. Martha is far better known as Calamity Jane, the cowgirl.

Martha was born in 1852 in Princeton, Missouri, the oldest of six children. In an autobiography that is filled with tall tales, Martha wrote that while she was still a child, she became an expert horsewoman. She said that she could control "even the most vicious and stubborn of horses."

Martha's family migrated west in 1865. Martha boasted that the treacherous trip was fun. While the men in her group struggled to pick their way on horseback across rain-swollen rivers, Martha supposedly swam her pony back and forth several times, "merely to amuse myself."

In later life, Martha wrote, she became a Pony Express rider, and safely carried the mail across "the most dangerous

Around 1870, Calamity Jane met another legendary figure from the Old West, Wild Bill Hickok. A former lawman, Hickok was a gambler and showman. True to his nickname, he had a wild personality. Historians disagree on whether Calamity ever married Wild Bill. There is also some confusion over whether the two had a child together. But they were certainly friends.

In 1876, Calamity and Wild Bill were in a town called Deadwood, in the Dakota Territory. Bill was playing poker in a saloon when a man named Jack McCall shot him dead. In her autobiography, Calamity wrote that she rushed to the saloon as soon as she heard the news. "I at once started to look for the assassin and found him at Shurdy's butcher shop," Calamity wrote. In her haste, she had left her guns on her bedpost, so she grabbed a meat cleaver at the butcher's shop, "and made him throw up his hands." She held McCall at cleaver-point, she claimed, until he was taken away and locked inside a log cabin. About seven months later, McCall was hanged for the murder of Wild Bill Hickok.

Calamity eventually went on tour, telling about her wild life. She always talked about her days with Bill, and shortly before she died in 1903, Calamity asked that she be buried next to Bill. The two legends of the West are buried next to one another in Deadwood.

route in the Black Hills." Another time, she said, she happened upon a team of horses hitched to a stagecoach whose driver had been shot dead by Indians. Martha claimed that she climbed into the driver's seat and drove the stagecoach into town.

These stories were well known in the Old West; but they probably did not happen. Instead, the truth of Martha's life is very sad. Her mother died on that 1865 trip west. Her father died after the family reached Salt Lake City. Her brothers and sisters were sent to live with other families, and young Martha was left to fend for herself.

Martha worked at any job she could find. According to the legend she created herself in her own autobiography, Martha eventually joined the famous General George Custer, and worked for him as a scout. Again, the story is most likely false, but Martha made it sound exciting. "When I joined Custer I donned the uniform of a soldier," she wrote. "It was a bit awkward at first but I soon got to be perfectly at home in men's clothes."

A few years later, she said, she was in the middle of a battle against a group of Native Americans, when her commander, a Captain Egan, was shot. Martha saw that Egan was about to fall from his horse. "I turned my horse and galloped back with all haste to his side," Martha wrote, "and got there in time to catch him as he was falling. I lifted him onto my horse in front of me, and succeeded in getting him safely to the fort."

According to Martha, Egan then named her "Calamity Jane." It was a strange name, since "calamity" means "disaster." But the name was also interesting and catchy. It drew attention. It was the perfect name for Martha's part in a new role for Western women: making and spreading the myth of the Old West.

🔥 Laura Ingalls Wilder (inset), a woman who grew up on the frontier during the second half of the 19th century, wrote about her life in the West in such books as *Little House in the Big Woods*, *Little House on the Prairie*, and *By the Shores of Silver Lake*. In the 1980s her experiences were made into a popular television show, *Little House on the Prairie*, the cast of which is pictured here.

6

TELLING THE TALE

LESS THAN 90 YEARS AFTER SACAGAWEA HELPED LEWIS AND CLARK ON THEIR HISTORIC expedition, the West was a bustling, established land. It had its own way of life, its own legends and myths. Promoters and showmen began to retell those legends in books and in shows. Soon, the West was more than just a place; it was also an image that had a special feeling in people's minds.

Calamity Jane was among the women who helped form the image of the Old West. She wrote her autobiography and sold it at fairs. Even though the book was filled with outrageous tall tales, people believed it. They thought of Calamity Jane as a sort of super-cowgirl. Calamity became even more famous when she joined Buffalo Bill's Wild West Show, a touring show that was very much like a Western-themed circus, with live buffalo and a Pony Express race.

Still, Calamity had a rough life. She drank a lot and got into fights. She lost various jobs. When she died of pneumonia in 1903, she was very poor.

The showman Buffalo Bill Cody, meanwhile, had another female star who was even more famous than Calamity Jane. Her name was Annie Oakley. She was an amazingly talented sharpshooter.

Annie's real name was Phoebe Ann Moses. Like Calamity Jane, little Phoebe had a sad early life. Her father died when she was six, and afterward, Phoebe's mother had a hard time caring for the family. Phoebe was sent to live for a while in foster homes. She later moved back in with her mother, who was remarried. Phoebe helped support the family with her shooting.

For nearly 25 years, Buffalo Bill's Wild West Show was a very popular entertainment. During 17 of those years, Annie Oakley was one of the show's most popular performers.

MARRIED MUM ?   NO SIR!

👆 The arrival of a single woman in a frontier town was a cause for celebration, as this woodcut cartoon shows. It was uncommon for an unmarried woman to venture west, and the population was heavily male for a long time.

Word quickly spread that the teenaged Phoebe could outshoot any man. Phoebe started to appear in sharpshooting competitions. She married one of the men she defeated, a professional sharpshooter named Frank Butler. Phoebe became known as Annie Oakley, and she and Frank went on tour together. Annie was so good with a gun, she could shoot a cigarette from Frank's lips.

Annie joined Buffalo Bill's Wild West Show. She did one trick in which she would turn her back on her target; aim by

During World War I, Annie Oakley, the famous sharpshooter from the Old West, gave shooting demonstrations to U.S. troops.

looking at the target's reflection in a knife blade; and shoot by firing over her shoulder. The audience was amazed. So, too, was the famous Sioux chief, Sitting Bull, who announced he had adopted Annie and named her "Little Sureshot."

Annie did a number of shooting tricks that seemed almost impossible. She twirled a *lariat* with one hand, and shot with the other. She shot glass balls out of the air. She shot a hole through a coin her husband held in his fingers.

Annie and the Wild West show went to Britain. The Grand Duke Michael of Russia was in Britain at the time, and he challenged Annie to a shooting match. Annie won. Buffalo Bill's group then went to Paris and performed near the Eiffel Tower, which had only just been completed. The French president supposedly offered Annie a place in the French Army. In Germany, Annie was asked to do her cigarette trick with a member of the German royal family holding the cigarette in his mouth.

Back in the United States, Annie was in a bad train wreck. It was two years before she could walk again; and even then, she had a limp. Sometime later, Annie was in yet another wreck, in an automobile. This time, she would not walk or shoot again.

Annie died a famous woman in 1926, and her legend lives on. To this day, one of the most popular Broadway musicals is *Annie, Get Your Gun*, about the life and times of the girl who was born Phoebe Ann Moses.

In their different ways, Calamity Jane and Annie Oakley helped spread the image of a wild and untamable West. Another woman spread a far different image, of a West that placed a high value on home and family.

Laura Ingalls Wilder was still a baby when her family migrated from Wisconsin to Missouri in 1868. Laura's family moved many times through what was then known as Indian Territory, in the present day states of Iowa, Kansas, Minnesota, and South Dakota. The family endured adversity and risk. When Laura grew up and got married, her adventures continued.

As an adult, Laura published her first book, *Little House in the Big Woods*, based on her childhood. Laura wrote more books, which became known as the *Little House on the Prairie* series. Girls and boys still enjoy Laura's books.

Laura Ingalls Wilder began to write at the urging of her daughter Rose, a journalist in San Francisco. Laura called her first book *When Grandma Was a Little Girl*. Laura's publisher changed the title to *Little House in the Big Woods*.

After Annie Oakley married Frank Butler, she traveled alongside him as he toured the country, giving shooting exhibitions. At first, Annie did not appear on stage. Frank already had an assistant who used to go on stage with him.

One night in 1883, Frank's assistant got sick right before the show started. Frank needed a substitute. He asked Annie to fill in for the assistant. Annie did the assistant's trick, and the audience was amazed by her skill. After that night, Annie became part of Frank's show.

Eventually, Frank realized that people only wanted to see Annie. In 1884, Frank stopped performing and became Annie's manager. He thought of tricks for her to perform, and helped decide where she should appear.

One of Annie's tricks was to shoot the middle out of a playing card. The shot-out cards looked like theater tickets that had been punched by a ticket-taker. People started to call punched-out theater tickets "Annie Oakleys."

Annie became so popular that she earned a huge income. When the average American was earning less than $500 per year, Annie made $150 a week.

When Frank and Annie retired, they were able to buy a home in Maryland. She wrote her autobiography, *Powders I Have Used*, in 1914. Frank and Annie eventually moved to North Carolina, then back to Ohio. On November 3, 1926, Annie died. Frank Butler died 18 days after his wife of 40 years.

The women of settled in the West helped to change the entire nation. As more women moved onto the western plains during the 1870s and 1880s, they brought with them the temperance movement. The word "temperance" means self-restraint in the face of temptation or desire. Those involved in the temperance movement wanted to prohibit the manufacture and sale of alcohol, so that people could restrain themselves from drinking.

The movement grew during the mid-19th century. It was often associated with the women's rights movement. In 1846 Maine passed the first state law banning alcohol. After the Civil War, two major temperance organizations emerged, the National Prohibition Party in 1869 and the Women's Christian Temperance Union (WCTU) in 1874. The temperance movement grew in strength in the Midwest and west, in part thanks to the leadership of a Kansas settler named Carry Nation (1846–1911).

Nation's first husband was an alcoholic; his death turned her against alcohol and saloons where it was served. She gained fame by showing up at taverns and saloons, yelling at the customers, and causing as much damage as she could with a hatchet. Nation was a large woman, nearly 6 feet tall and weighing 175 pounds, and she terrorized barkeepers throughout Kansas.

Illness forced Carry Nation to give up the battle against alcohol in the early 1900s. She died on June 9, 1911, at her home in Leavenworth, Kansas. Eight years after her death, in 1919, the Nineteenth Amendment to the U.S. Constitution, prohibiting the manufacture and sale of alcohol, became the law of the land.

Women also contributed to a growing movement for safer workplaces and better working conditions for both men and women, as well as child labor regulations. By 1896, many of the western states had outlawed child labor and placed restrictions on the length of the work day for adults. Utah, for example, passed a law setting the work day at eight hours for miners. Settlement houses for poor immigrants were established in Los Angeles and other California cities, just a few years after the first such houses sprang up in New York and on the east coast.

Today, we can only imagine what life must have been like for women in the Old West. Old journals and letters tell us that women lived through much difficulty and adventure. The excitement must have been intense—but it was also fairly short lived. By 1890, the frontier days were practically over.

At least one young woman was bored. Maude C. Parker lived with her father in California, and in 1890, Maude kept a small, leather-bound diary. In some of her entries, Maude wrote simply, "Did the same as usual." She complained that she had "no pretty hat, no dress, never any gloves." Elsewhere, she wrote, "I am just so tired of it all. This living in a shanty goes dreadfully against the grain."

Finally, Maude found the answer to her boring life: "I'll pick myself up and go to China, that's what I'll do." The Wild West had become too tame; a Western woman was forced to look elsewhere for excitement!

GLOSSARY

Antibiotic
A substance that is able to kill or weaken bacteria in the body.

Blacksmith
An ironworker.

Bounty hunter
A person who tracks down criminals for a reward.

Buckskin
A soft light-colored leather that originally was made from the skin of a male deer.

Campaign
A series of events, including rallies and speeches, that are intended to persuade voters to vote for a particular politician or party.

Emigrant
A person who leaves his or her home to live somewhere else.

Entrepreneur
A person who finances a new business venture, often willing to take risks in order to make a profit.

Frontier
The region on the edge of settled and civilized land.

Juries
Groups of people who are sworn to use their best judgment to make a legal verdict on a court case.

Justice of the peace
A local law person, who is able to decide minor court cases, send more serious crimes to trial, and perform marriages.

Lariat
A lasso; a rope with a noose on the end.

Legislator

A lawmaker.

Levee

A natural or artificial embankment alongside a river that prevents flooding.

Marshals

Law officers appointed to a particular district; similar to a sheriff.

Midwife

A woman who helps a pregnant woman give birth to her child.

Migration

Moving from one area to another.

Posse

A group of people summoned by the sheriff to help keep the peace.

Score

A group of twenty things or people.

Status

Rank or prestige.

Suffrage

The right to vote in public elections.

Town crier

A person who walks around town shouting out the news.

TIMELINE

1804

Indian teenager Sacagawea joins the Lewis and Clark expedition as a guide.

1836

Narcissa Whitman heads west with her husband to establish a mission in Oregon Territory.

1846

Tabitha Brown begins her journey to Oregon via covered wagon.

1847

Tabitha Brown co-founds the Orphan Asylum in Forest Grove; the school later becomes Pacific University.

1859

Margaret McNeil joins other Mormons in migrating west on foot. Margaret has the added burden of carrying her sick little brother on her back.

1870

Esther Morris becomes the first woman to be named a justice of the peace, in South Pass City, Wyoming Territory.

1871

Abigail Scott Duniway starts publishing her own weekly newspaper, the *New Northwest*, advocating women's rights.

1882

Belle Starr is charged with horse theft in Arkansas; after 47 years of separation, former slave Clara Brown is reunited with her long-lost daughter.

1885

Former slave Mary Fields arrives in Cascade, Montana, to join her childhood friend, a nun named Mother Amadeus; shooting sensation Phoebe Ann Moses, calling herself Annie Oakley, joins Buffalo Bill Cody's Wild West Show.

1889

Belle Starr, the Bandit Queen, is shot to death in Arkansas.

1890

Wyoming becomes the first state in the Union to legalize voting for women.

1892

Martha Jane Cannary, calling herself Calamity Jane, joins Buffalo Bill Cody's Wild West Show.

1899

Pearl Hart disguises herself as a man and joins her friend Joe Boot in robbing a stagecoach in Arizona.

1910

Washington State women earn the right to vote.

1912

Oregon women win the right to vote.

FURTHER READING

Burns, Ken, and Dayton Duncan. *Lewis and Clark: The Journey of the Corps of Discovery, an Illustrated History*. New York: Alfred A. Knopf, 1997.

Butruille, Susan G. *Women's Voices From the Oregon Trail*. Boise, Idaho: Tamarack Books, 1993.

Holmes, Kenneth L., ed. *Covered Wagon Women: Diaries and Letters from the Western Trails, 1850*: Volume 1. Lincoln: University of Nebraska Press, 1996.

———. *Covered Wagon Women: Diaries and Letters from the Western Plains, 1840-1849: Volume 2*. Lincoln: University of Nebraska Press, 1995.

Levy, Jo Ann. *They Saw the Elephant: Women in the California Gold Rush*. Hamden, Conn.: Archon Books, 1990.

Schlissel, Lillian. *Women's Diaries of the Westward Journey*. New York: Schocken Books, 1982.

Stefoff, Rebecca. *Women Pioneers*. New York: Facts on File, 1995.

Wright, Mike. *What They Didn't Teach You About the Wild West*. Novato, Calif.: Presidio Press, 2000.

INTERNET RESOURCES

Women in the West

http://www.pbs.org/weta/thewest/

http://www.rootsweb.com/~nwa/pioneer.html

http://www.over-land.com/westpers2.html

http://www.wowmuseum.org/erc/edlos.html

http://www.library.csi.cuny.edu/westweb/pages/women.html

Belle Starr and Pearl Hart

http://www.thehistorynet.com/WildWest/articles/1997/08972_text.htm

http://members2.gotnet.net/rcbusman/women/starr.htm

http://www.geocities.com/SouthBeach/Marina/2057/Pearl_Bywater.html

http://members2.gotnet.net/rcbusman/women/hart.html

Annie Oakley

http://www.ormiston.com/annieoakley/

http://www.cowgirls.com/dream/cowgals/oakley.htm

http://pages.prodigy.com/legends/annie.htm

Laura Ingalls Wilder

http://www.missourichamber.com/mansfield/tours.htm

http://www.liwms.com/

http://www.galegroup.com/freresrc/womenhst/bio/wilderx.htm

http://www.vvv.com/~jenslegg/

INDEX

PHOTO CREDITS

ABOUT THE AUTHOR

Susan Katz Keating is a freelance writer and educator. A former newspaper reporter and editor, her work has appeared in *Readers Digest*, *George*, the *New York Times*, and other publications. She is the author of *Prisoners of Hope: Exploiting the POW/MIA Myth in America* (Random House), named Best Book on the Vietnam War for 1994 by the American War Library. She is the mother of three children and lives with her family in Virginia.